Sing a Song of People

by Lois Lenski

Illustrated by Giles Laroche

Little, Brown and Company
Boston   New York   Toronto   London

First Paperback Edition

The text of "Sing a Song of People" first appeared in *The Life I Live* by Lois
Lenski, and is reprinted here by arrangement with The Lois Lenski Covey
Foundation, Inc.

Library of Congress Cataloging-in-Publication Data
Lenski, Lois
   Sing a song of people.

   Summary: Depicts the pleasures of city life, people alone and in crowds,
smiling and hurrying, on the sidewalk, bus, and subway.
   [1. City and town life–Fiction. 2. Stories in
rhyme] I. Laroche, Giles, ill. II. Title.
PZ8.3.L546Si 1987   [E]   86-20873
ISBN 0-316-52074-8 (hc)
ISBN 0-316-52070-5 (pb)
10   9   8   7   6   5   4   3

Designed by Trisha Hanlon

WOR

Published simultaneously in Canada
by Little, Brown & Company (Canada) Limited

Printed in the United States of America

For Andrea and Beth

Sing a song of people
Walking fast or slow;

People in the city,
Up and down they go.

People on the sidewalk,

People on the bus;

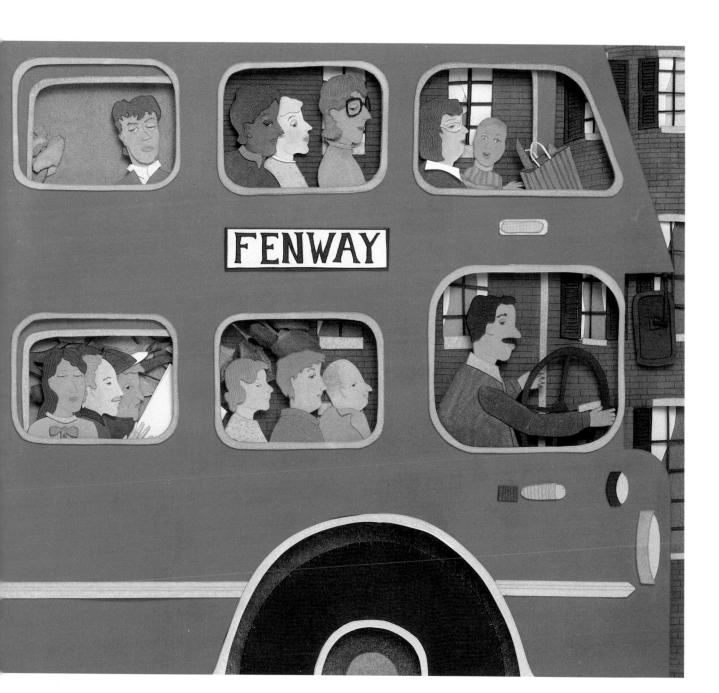

People passing, passing,

In back and front of us.

People on the subway
Underneath the ground;

People riding taxis
Round and round and round.

People with their hats on,

Going in the doors;

People with umbrellas
When it rains and pours.

People in tall buildings

And in stores below;

Riding in elevators
Up and down they go.

People walking singly,

People in a crowd;

People saying nothing,
People talking loud.

People laughing, smiling,

Grumpy people too;

People who just hurry
And never look at you!

Sing a song of people
Who like to come and go;

Sing of city people
You see but never know!